The Little Aussie Adventurers

A Friendship Begins

by Anita Forbes and Natalie Jane Parker

Work hard! Concentrate! Follow the line! Work hard! Concentrate! Follow the line!

Flynn loved being an ant — most of the time — but sometimes he got very tired of working. So one day he crept away from his family and found a big, green gum leaf to lie on.

"I think I will relax for a while," he thought to himself. Flynn was almost asleep when . . .

Whoosh!

. . . a huge hot gust of wind picked up the leaf and tossed it around and around in the air. Flynn held on tight and screamed with all his might. The leaf travelled a very long way until . . .

Kaplop!

Flynn and the leaf
landed on the ground.

Flynn was dizzy. He was very dizzy! At last, when his head stopped spinning, he stood up and looked around.

There before him were flowers of every kind and colour imaginable. It was such a beautiful place.

Just then, Flynn noticed one of the leaves glistening in the sun. To his surprise, the leaf spoke:

"Hi," it said. "I'm Benny." Flynn looked closer — it wasn't a leaf at all!

"Hello," said Flynn to Benny the beetle. "I think I'm lost. I was asleep on a leaf when the wind carried me here. Please can you help me find my way home?"

Benny was happy to help, so together they set off in search of Flynn's home.

Not far into their journey they met Wally Wallaby.

"I'm sure my family will be missing me," said Flynn.
"Do you know where my home could be?"

"I'm not sure," said Wally. "Is it near this big gum tree?
Why don't you go up and see?"

So Benny and Flynn climbed the tall gum tree as fast as their little legs could carry them.

There in the fork of the tree they met Eucalypta, the koala.

"I'm sure my family will be missing me," said Flynn to Eucalypta. "Do you know where my home could be?"

Eucalypta replied in a rather slow and sleepy voice:

"I sleep and eat leaves all day. I don't know, but you could ask Matthew the magpie."

Matthew came swooping down from the branches above and was quick to reply . . .

"Well, if you're looking for an ant hill it's not going to be up this tree! Try looking on the ground," he said. But, just as he was taking off again, he accidently knocked the branch that Benny and Flynn were sitting on.

"Auggh-h-h!" called Benny, losing his balance. He tried to grab onto the branch but missed. He wished very hard that he could fly. Then, suddenly, he stopped falling.

"Look, Flynn, look!" he called. "I'm flying! I've got wings and I'm flying! Whe-e-e-e-eee!" But Flynn was bouncing from leaf to leaf all the way down to the ground . . .

Flynn got up off the ground, and he and Benny set off once more in search of his home.

Before long, they ran into Emma the emu. "I'm sure my family will be missing me," said Flynn. "Do you know where my home could be?" "I haven't seen your home," said Emma, "but perhaps you should keep looking along this path."

Benny and Flynn walked and walked. Soon it began to get dark, so they decided to rest. They found some leaves to hide beneath and quickly fell asleep.

In the middle of the night Flynn woke up. He was scared. He was not used to sleeping in a different place. He liked his new friend Benny, but he missed his family.

"Benny! Wake up! Let's go!" he said. "I want to find my family!" So Benny and Flynn got up and set off into the night.

After a while, they came to a creek and decided to cross to the other side.

Even though Benny could fly, he decided to jump from rock to rock across the creek like Flynn. It was fun! They were just getting the hang of it when . . .

"An earthquake!" yelled Flynn. The rock he had landed on was moving. Just then, a head appeared out of the water. Flynn had landed on Tyler the turtle.

"What's going on?" asked Tyler.

"I really miss my father and mother, and we need to get from this side of the creek to the other," explained Flynn.

"Well, it will soon be day," said Tyler, "so let me take you the rest of the way."

When they were safely on the other side of the creek, they thanked Tyler and set off again in search of Flynn's home. Very soon they met Blue, the red-eyed green tree frog.

"I'm sure my family will be missing me," said Flynn once more. "Do you know where my home could be?"

"It's a bit too muddy for an ant hill around here," said Blue. "Why don't you look for some dry ground?"

So Benny and Flynn set off once more. They walked and walked and walked, and eventually, just as the sun was rising, Flynn saw a familiar sight . . .

Flynn could see his family — still working hard and still in line.
He was so glad to see them and his ant hill home.

And Flynn's family was so happy to see him again!

They had been very worried about him, but now for the first time ever they stopped work to celebrate his return.

Benny was welcomed as if he were part of their family, and they all had a wonderful party.